RAINBOW magic

The Twilight Fairies

Special thanks
to Narinder Dhami

ORCHARD BOOKS
338 Euston Road, London NW1 3BH
Orchard Books Australia
Level 17/207 Kent Street, Sydney, NSW 2000
A Paperback Original

First published in 2010 by Orchard Books

HiT entertainment

A CIP catalogue record for this book is available
from the British Library.

ISBN 978 1 40830 906 3

1 3 5 7 9 10 8 6 4 2

Printed in China by Imago

The paper and board used in this paperback are natural recyclable
products made from wood grown in sustainable forests. The
manufacturing processes conform to the environmental regulations
of the country of origin.

Orchard Books is a division of Hachette Children's Books,
an Hachette UK company

www.hachette.co.uk

Ava
the Sunset
Fairy

by Daisy Meadows

ORCHARD BOOKS

www.rainbowmagic.co.uk

The Twilight Fairies' magical powers
Bring harmony to the night-time hours.
But now their magic belongs to me,
And I'll cause chaos, you shall see!

Sunset, moonlight and starlight too,
There'll be no more sweet dreams for you,
From evening dusk to morning light
I am the master of the night!

Contents

Strange Sunset

"Look, Kirsty!" Rachel Walker said
excitedly to her best friend, Kirsty Tate.
It was a warm summer's evening, and the
girls were standing on the deck of a little
red and white ferry as it chugged its way
along the winding river. "I don't think
we're far from Camp Stargaze now."

Kirsty looked where Rachel was pointing and saw a wooden sign on the river bank. The sign was in the shape of an arrow pointing downriver and it said: *This way to Camp Stargaze.*

"Brilliant!" Kirsty beamed at Rachel. "I'm *really* looking forward to this holiday."

The girls and their parents were spending a week of the summer break at Camp Stargaze together. Kirsty and Rachel were thrilled because although they were best friends, they didn't live near each other. So they loved meeting up in their school holidays whenever they could.

"Not far to go now, girls," called Mr Walker, Rachel's dad. He was leaning on the side of the boat with Mrs Walker

and Mr and Mrs Tate, watching the
beautiful countryside pass by. The river
was surrounded by open fields and gently
rolling hills, with green woodlands here
and there.

"Oh, look, girls!" Mrs Tate exclaimed,
gazing up at the sky. "The sun is setting.
Isn't it lovely?"

All the passengers on deck, including
Rachel and Kirsty, looked upwards, too.
The sun was just beginning to sink very
slowly in the sky, streaking the blue with
long ribbons of gold, orange and pink.
The light reflected downwards onto the
river and the fields, bathing everything
in a soft glow and turning the water to
liquid gold.

"It's magical!" Rachel breathed, her eyes wide. Then she glanced at Kirsty and flashed her a secret smile.

Kirsty grinned back, knowing exactly what Rachel was thinking. She and Rachel knew more about magic than anyone else in the whole world because they were friends with the fairies! The girls had visited Fairyland many times and had helped out their magical friends whenever they were in trouble. The fairies' biggest enemy was mean, grumpy Jack Frost, who was always trying to cause trouble in Fairyland and in the human world. Rachel and Kirsty were never quite sure what tricks Jack Frost and his goblin servants would get up to next!

Suddenly Kirsty blinked a little. For a moment she'd thought the gold, orange and pink colours of the setting sun were fading and changing into something different.

I must be imagining it, Kirsty thought. But then she looked again and was horrified to see that she was right. The beautiful colours *were* changing before Kirsty's very eyes.

"What's happening?" Rachel asked. She'd noticed exactly the same thing, and so had everyone else on board.

They were all staring up at the sky
in surprise.

"Look at the sunset," Kirsty
cried. "It's turning *green!*"
A few seconds later,
all the gold, pink
and orange
had vanished
completely.
Now the light
of the sunset
was casting a
strange, spooky
green glow on the
landscape around it.
"Everything's green!"
Kirsty went on in a shocked
voice. "The sun, the fields, the
ferry – everything."

"And so are *we!*" Rachel pointed out, staring at Kirsty. All of the passengers, including the girls and their parents, were bathed in the same emerald-coloured glow.

"We look like Jack Frost's goblins!" Kirsty whispered.

The girls' parents and the other grown-ups on the ferry were discussing what could have caused the strange sunset.

"Maybe it's just a trick of the light shining through the clouds," Mr Tate suggested.

"Or perhaps the sunset is reflecting off the river and the fields and picking up that green colour," said Mrs Walker.

Looking puzzled, Rachel glanced at Kirsty. "I think there's something very strange going on here, Kirsty," she murmured.

"So do I," Kirsty agreed. "I wonder if it could be something *magical*?"

Twilight Tent

"Here we are," called the captain of the ferry as it came in to dock at a small wooden jetty. "Welcome to Camp Stargaze."

Rachel and Kirsty stared eagerly at the pretty campsite as they waited for their turn to climb off the ferry.

There was a sign with *Welcome to Camp Stargaze* painted on it in silver letters, and beyond that the girls could see large tents pitched here and there on the grass next to a green woodland. The tents all had different names on wooden signs outside the entrances. They were surrounded by colourful flowerbeds, and a little sparkling stream flowed through the campsite on its way to the river. There were plenty of open spaces for games and activities, and lots of picnic

tables scattered about. The girls were also excited to see a small white building with a dome on top of it.

"Remember I told you this area was chosen for the camp because you can get really clear views of the night sky and constellations from here?" Mrs Tate reminded Rachel and Kirsty. "Well, that white building is the observatory. There's a telescope inside it to look at the stars."

"I can't wait!" Rachel said with a grin, and Kirsty nodded in agreement.

"Camp Stargaze looks great, doesn't it, girls?" Mr Walker remarked as they picked up their luggage. "It's a shame this sunset is making everything turn green, though!"

The camp leaders were waiting on the jetty with their clipboards to check everyone in. As the Walkers and the Tates climbed off the ferry, one of the leaders stepped forward.

"Hi, I'm Peter," he said with a smile. "Welcome to Camp Stargaze. Now, let's find out which tent you'll be staying in."

Peter checked his clipboard and told the Walkers and Tates that they were in the Twilight Tent. Then he gave them a map of the campsite and pointed them in the right direction.

"The Twilight Tent," Rachel repeated as they walked past the welcome sign and into the camp. There were lots of other families settling in and some, like the Walkers and Tates, milling around searching for their tents. "That sounds lovely, Kirsty."

"Is it this one?" Kirsty stopped to peer at a sign outside a pale cream-coloured tent. "Oh no, this is the Moonlight Tent."

"There it is!" Rachel said excitedly as she spotted a sign saying *The Twilight Tent.*

The girls were thrilled to see that their tent was the colour of the night sky, a deep midnight blue, and scattered with tiny silver stars. The tent was enormous and most of it had been partitioned off into three separate sleeping areas, one bedroom for each set of parents and one for Rachel and Kirsty to share. There was also a small kitchen and living-area at the front of the tent.

"This is great!" Kirsty beamed at Rachel as they tried out the camp beds in their bedroom. "The tent's almost as big as a house."

Mrs Walker popped her head in at that moment. "There's a shower and toilet block just a short walk away," she told them. "Why don't you two go and explore the rest of the camp while we do the unpacking? We'll see you for the barbecue later."

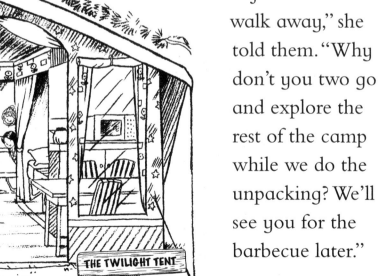

THE TWILIGHT TENT

"OK, Mum," Rachel said. "Let's go, Kirsty."

The girls left their bags in the bedroom and wandered out into the campsite. Just outside their tent, a group of children of all ages were clustered around Peter, the camp leader the girls had already met. They were staring up at the sky which was still green. Rachel and Kirsty went to join them.

"Isn't it strange how the sun hasn't set yet?" Peter was saying with a frown. "It should be dark by now."

The girls had been so excited about arriving at Camp Stargaze, they hadn't really noticed that the sun had stopped setting. Now, though, they could see that the sun didn't seem to have sunk any lower in the green sky.

"Have you had a green sunset here before, Peter?" asked one of the boys in the group.

Peter shook his head. "Never!" he replied. "I have no idea what's causing it."

Kirsty glanced at Rachel. "There really *is* something weird going on," she remarked.

Rachel did not reply because her eye had suddenly been caught by a tiny patch of golden light in the middle of the green sunset. As she stared at it, the light seemed to grow brighter and more sparkly.

"Kirsty!" Rachel nudged her friend. "Can you see that little gleam of light among the green?"

Kirsty looked and nodded. "Is it a star?" she asked.

As Rachel and Kirsty watched in wonder, they saw the sparkling patch of sunset swirl down from the sky and swoop towards the river. None of the other campers noticed.

"Quick, let's go and find out what it is!" Rachel whispered to Kirsty.

The girls ran down to the bank of the river just as the dazzling light skimmed quickly across the water towards them. Then it landed in a shimmer of sparkles on top of the *Welcome to Camp Stargaze* sign.

"Kirsty!" Rachel cried, her face full of excitement. "It's a fairy!"

Jack Frost's Plan

The tiny fairy was out of breath after her speedy flight. She looked around to check that none of the other campers could see her, and then she waved at Rachel and Kirsty.

"Hi, girls," she panted, "We haven't met before, but I've seen you in Fairyland lots of times! I'm Ava the Sunset Fairy, one of the Twilight Fairies."

Thrilled, Rachel and Kirsty rushed over to Ava, who fluttered down to perch on Kirsty's shoulder. Ava wore a beaded dress in soft, sunset shades of pink and orange, and sparkly, ankle-strap ballet shoes. Her long, wavy auburn hair was pinned back from her face with a glittery pink clip.

"What are you doing here, Ava?" Kirsty asked.

"Is it because of this green sunset?" Rachel wanted to know.

Ava's face fell. "Yes, girls," she said sadly. "I can't *believe* what Jack Frost has done!"

Rachel and Kirsty glanced at each other in horror.

"Jack Frost's up to his old tricks *again*?!" Rachel groaned.

"Girls, will you help me and the other Twilight Fairies to put things right?" Ava asked them anxiously. "We can't do it without you."

Immediately Rachel and Kirsty nodded.

"What happened, Ava?" said Kirsty.

Ava sighed. "It's a long story, so the quickest way to explain it all is if you come back to Fairyland with me," she replied.

"You can meet the other six Twilight Fairies, and we can show you what happened. Will you come, girls?"

"Of course we will!" Rachel and Kirsty cried. The girls knew that, as always,

time would stand still while they were
in Fairyland, so their parents would not
worry about them.

Looking very relieved, Ava lifted her
wand and surrounded the two girls with
a cloud of magical fairy dust. Rachel
and Kirsty closed their eyes as they were
whisked off their feet, and then they felt
themselves rushing through the air at
great speed.

"Here we are," Ava called. "Welcome
to Fairyland again, girls."

Rachel and Kirsty opened their eyes.
They were standing in the beautiful
gardens of the Fairyland Palace, and
waiting to greet them were King Oberon,
Queen Titania and six other fairies.

"Girls, once again you've answered
our call for help," Queen Titania said

gratefully, moving forward to hug first Rachel and then Kirsty. "We're *so* glad to see you."

"And so are the Twilight Fairies," King Oberon added, nodding at the six fairies standing beside him.

"You've already met Ava, and here are Lexi the Firefly Fairy, Zara the Starlight Fairy, Morgan the Midnight Fairy, Yasmin the Night Owl Fairy, Maisie the Moonbeam Fairy and Sabrina the Sweet Dreams Fairy."

"Our Twilight Fairies make sure everything that happens between dusk and dawn goes smoothly, in both the fairy and human worlds," explained Queen Titania. "But now naughty Jack Frost and his goblins have ruined the night-time!"

"How?" Kirsty asked.

"We'll show you exactly what happened in the Seeing Pool," Ava said.

The king and queen led the way through the gardens to the magical pool. The surface of the water was smooth and glass-like, but

when Queen Titania waved her wand over it, the pool began to ripple and swirl gently. A few seconds later, pictures began to appear in the water. Rachel and Kirsty stared closely and saw a beautiful pink and gold bedroom with seven little beds.

"This is the Twilight Fairies' bedroom inside the palace," Ava told them. The door opened and Ava and the other six fairies fluttered into their bedroom. The girls noticed that each fairy was holding a small, satin drawstring bag, all of them different colours.

"Every one of us has a bag filled with our own special kind of magic dust," Ava went on. "We keep them under our pillows, as you can see."

The fairies were now slipping their magical bags underneath their silk pillowcases. Then, looking excited, they hurried out of the bedroom again.

"We were on our way to a Twilight Party under the stars last night with all our fairy friends," Ava explained. "But look what happened while we were gone…"

Rachel and Kirsty gazed at the Seeing Pool. Suddenly, Jack Frost and a crowd of goblins whizzed through the open window, riding on a blast of icy wind.

"I want those bags!" Jack Frost yelled. "Hurry up and steal them before those silly Twilight Fairies come back!"

The goblins jumped down and scattered in all directions. They threw the pillows off the beds and grabbed the satin bags, holding them up triumphantly to show Jack Frost.

Then one of the goblins picked up a pillow with his free hand and, chuckling to himself, he smacked the goblin closest around the head with it.

The second goblin roared with fury and snatched another pillow to hit him back.

Soon all the goblins were having a pillow fight. They were whacking each other so hard that the pillows burst, and tiny, downy white feathers flew everywhere, making a huge mess. Rachel and Kirsty glanced at each other in dismay.

"Enough!" Jack Frost roared furiously. All the goblins dropped their pillows, looking very sheepish, and stood clutching the bags.

"With the Twilight Fairies' magic, I can cause night-time chaos *everywhere*," Jack Frost gloated. "But we must keep the bags hidden away in the human world."

He pointed his wand at the goblins. An ice bolt sped towards them, sweeping the goblins off their feet.

Then it zoomed out of the window, taking the goblins and the Twilight Fairies' magical bags with it.

Jack Frost looked extremely pleased with himself.

"Usually I hate the night-time," he muttered. "But now I can control everything that happens between dusk and dawn, things are going to be different!" And with a cackle of icy laughter, he, too, whizzed out of the window and back to his Ice Castle.

"Without our special magic, nothing will go right between the evening and the morning!" Ava told Rachel and Kirsty. "Will you help me find my bag of sunbeam dust, girls?"

Rachel and Kirsty nodded eagerly.

"But why does Jack Frost want to disrupt the night-time so much?" asked Kirsty, looking puzzled.

"We don't know," Queen Titania replied. "But we must *stop* him!" She lifted her sparkling wand. "Girls, I shall send you and Ava straight back to Camp Stargaze now. The bags will have become bigger in the human world, so they'll be easier to spot. Good luck with your quest."

"Good luck!" echoed the other fairies

as the queen showered Ava and the girls with magic fairy dust.

Rachel and Kirsty waved at their friends, feeling very excited.

Another wonderful fairy adventure was about to begin!

Two Greedy Boys

Just a few seconds later, Rachel and
Kirsty were back at Camp Stargaze,
standing by the welcome sign. Ava was
hovering next to them. Everything was
still covered in the same green glow, and
the sun had remained high up in the sky.

Ava frowned. "The sun won't set again until I find my bag of sunbeam dust," she sighed. "I can sense it's around here *somewhere*."

"We'll do our best to find it, Ava," Kirsty promised.

"The barbecue's starting," Rachel said. The camp leaders had set up trestle tables and were putting big bowls of salad and plates of bread rolls on them. Meanwhile

Peter, wearing a chef's hat, was keeping watch over a large barbecue and flipping the grills and burgers every so often.

"We'd better go and find our parents," said Kirsty. "They'll be wondering where we are."

Ava nodded and fluttered out of sight into Rachel's pocket. The girls hurried across the campsite towards their parents, who were just joining the end of the queue for the barbecue.

"Ah, there you are, girls." Mr Tate handed Rachel and Kirsty a plate each. "We were wondering where you'd got to."

"This looks great, doesn't it?" Mrs Walker said, admiring the big bowls of different salads and heaps of brown and white soft rolls.

Rachel and Kirsty nodded.

"I hope this doesn't take *too* long, though," Rachel whispered to Kirsty as they waited in line. "I want to start looking for Ava's bag of sunbeam dust!"

But to the girls' dismay, the queue was moving very slowly indeed. Rachel and Kirsty soon realised that this was because of two boys who were just ahead of them.

The boys, wearing sunhats, big T-shirts and baggy combat shorts, were greedily helping themselves to lots of food from all the different bowls, and carrying as much as they could.

"They *are* hungry!" Kirsty murmured.

She and Rachel watched as the boys
wandered unsteadily over to the picnic
tables on the far side of the campsite,
clutching their armfuls of food.

Then Rachel nudged Kirsty.

"Look at their noses and their feet!" she
whispered in her friend's ear.

Kirsty stared at the two boys as they sat
down at the picnic table furthest away
from everyone else and began to tuck in.

They looked green, but so did everyone else at the camp because of the sunset glow. However, these two boys also had long pointed noses and very big feet.

"Goblins!" Kirsty murmured.

"I wonder if they have Ava's bag of sunbeam dust?" said Rachel. "We've got to find out, Kirsty!"

Rachel and Kirsty quickly collected their own supper and then asked their parents if they could sit with some of the other children.

Their parents agreed, so the girls hurried over to the picnic table next to the goblins. Some of the children they'd met earlier were there, and they were chatting about the activities at the camp. Rachel and Kirsty joined in, but at the same time they were listening to what the goblins at the next table were saying.

"Give that bread roll back!" one of the goblins yelled. "It's mine!"

"Shan't!" retorted the other goblin,

taking a big bite out of it.

The first goblin pulled a face at him. "Have you still got that bag of fairy dust in your pocket?" he demanded.

The girls glanced at each other.

"Of course I have," the second goblin said grumpily through a mouthful of bread roll. "I'm far too clever to lose something as important as *that*!" He shoved his hand into the pocket of his combat shorts, but then his face fell. "The bag's gone!" he groaned. "I must have dropped it."

"Let me see!" the other goblin demanded. He scrambled across the bench and grabbed his friend, turning his pockets inside-out. The other goblin roared in protest.

"You *have* lost it, you idiot!" the first goblin wailed, poking the other in the ribs with a breadstick. "What's Jack Frost going to say when he finds out? We're in big trouble."

Kirsty turned to Rachel. "We need to find Ava's bag of sunbeam dust before the goblins do!" she whispered.

In the Whispering Wood

"Let's eat our food and then we can start searching the campsite," Rachel suggested. The goblins continued to scoff their supper greedily, still grumbling about the loss of the sunbeam dust. Rachel and Kirsty finished eating, but before they had a chance to start their search, Peter called all the children together.

"Since the sun hasn't set yet, we can stay up a bit later and play a game," he announced. There were cheers at this. "How about hide and seek in the Whispering Wood?" And he pointed to the woodland at the edge of the campsite.

"Perfect!" Rachel murmured to Kirsty. "We'll be able to hunt for Ava's bag while we play, and no-one will guess what we're up to!"

"Off you go then." Peter covered his eyes and started counting.

"One, two, three…"

Rachel, Kirsty and the others ran towards the Whispering Wood. Kirsty glanced back and saw that the two goblins were still at the picnic table, stuffing themselves with food.

"At least the goblins won't be looking for the bag yet," she told Rachel. "They're too busy eating!"

Once the girls were in the wood, Ava popped her head out of Rachel's pocket. She checked that there was no-one around, and then flew out.

"Great work spotting those goblins, girls!" Ava cried. "I *know* my bag of sunbeam dust is very close by. We *must* find it."

Quickly Ava, Rachel and Kirsty began to search among the trees. Suddenly they heard Peter shout, "Coming, ready or not!"

Kirsty looked worried. "We'd better hide," she said. "If Peter finds us, we'll be out of the game and we'll have to go back to camp before we've searched the wood properly."

Kirsty and Rachel hurried towards a large, thick bush. As they reached it, Ava suddenly gave a squeak of alarm.

"There's already someone hiding there!" she whispered, diving out of sight behind Kirsty's hair.

Rachel and Kirsty saw Alex, one of the other campers, waving at them from behind the bush. "Come on," Alex said with a smile, beckoning to them, "There's plenty of room!"

The girls slipped behind the bush to join her. Almost immediately they heard footsteps.

"Ssh!" Alex put her finger to her lips. "This might be Peter."

But it wasn't. Rachel and Kirsty glanced at each other in dismay as they peered through the leaves and saw the outline of a pointy nose. It was a goblin, the one who'd lost the bag.

"Come and hide," Alex called to the goblin. "Peter's on his way!"

"I'm not playing this silly game," the goblin replied grumpily. "I'm looking for something very important!" And he went on his way.

"I can hear more footsteps," Alex warned Rachel and Kirsty.

A moment later Peter went past, but he didn't notice them. Alex gave a sigh of relief.

"I think I'll go and find my friend Katie and hide with her," she told the girls. "Do you want to come?"

"Thanks, Alex," Rachel replied with a smile, "but I think we'll stay here."

Alex ran off. Quickly Ava flew out from behind Kirsty's hair.

"Let's keep looking!" she said, urgently.

The three friends continued searching the woods. Rachel was concentrating so hard on looking around, she was startled when a rabbit ran past her. With a smile, she watched the rabbit lollop into his hole near the roots of a tree.

Then Rachel's heart began to thump with excitement. There, snagged on the roots of the tree, was a sparkling little satin drawstring bag.

"I've found it!" Rachel gasped.

Ava and Kirsty hurried over to Rachel, but before they could grab the bag, they heard footsteps. Immediately they all slipped behind the tree closest to them.

But to their horror, the goblin they'd seen
a little earlier had appeared.

"Yes!" the goblin crowed with glee as he
spotted the bag. "I knew I'd find it again!"

"We have to stop him—" Rachel began.

"Wait!" Kirsty clutched her arm.
"Someone's coming."

As the goblin went to pick up the bag,
Peter ran down the path.

"Got you!" he said with a smile,
grabbing the goblin by the arm.
"You're out!"

"Let me go!" the
goblin complained
as Peter led him
away. He hadn't
had a chance to
pick the bag up.
"I'm not playing!"

But Peter took no notice. Ava and the girls shared a relieved smile as Peter and the goblin disappeared.

"Now's our chance!" Ava whispered.

They rushed out from behind the tree. But before they reached the bag, they heard the sound of yet more footsteps.

"It might be Peter coming back," Ava pointed out. "Let me turn you into fairies, girls, so you won't be spotted!"

With one swish of Ava's wand, Kirsty and Rachel were scattered with fairy dust. Immediately they shrank down to Ava's size, using their

glittering fairy wings to zoom upwards
and hide behind the branch of a tree with
their friend.

"Oh, no!" Rachel gasped in horror. "It's
the *other* goblin!"

The second goblin began to search
around the trees while Ava and the girls
held their breath. Suddenly he spotted the
bag of sunbeam dust and gave a shout
of triumph.

"I've found it!" the goblin yelled. He grabbed the bag and jumped up and down with glee. "Hurrah! Now we won't be in trouble with Jack Frost after all!"

Suddenly there was the sound of someone running, and then the other goblin rushed through the trees.

"Look, I've found the magic bag," the second goblin proclaimed smugly, showing it off.

"Then let's get out of here right away!" the first goblin panted. "I've only just managed to escape from that silly man!"

"We have to get my bag back," Ava said anxiously as the two goblins hurried off. "What can we do, girls?"

"I think I have a plan!" Kirsty replied.

Green Dust

"Ava, maybe we could distract the goblins with *another* bag," Kirsty explained. "One that *really* catches their eye?"

Ava thought for a moment. "I can do that!" she said with a smile.

She flicked her wand, and a cloud of magical sparkles drifted down onto the path in front of the goblins. Instantly, a green satin bag appeared.

"Look!" the goblin with Ava's bag shouted. "Another bag – and it's *green*!"

The goblins picked the bag up and examined it closely.

"It's got a picture of two handsome goblins stitched on the front," said the goblin with Ava's bag. "Ooh, look – it's *US!*"

Ava and the girls tried not to laugh.

The other goblin opened the bag and a puff of green dust floated out.

"I like *this* bag much better," he said. "The green dust is just like the sunset."

"This must be the bag Jack Frost meant us to look after all along!" the goblin with Ava's bag agreed. "We'll leave the other one here and take *this* one instead." He was about to drop the bag of sunbeam dust on the path, when the other goblin clutched his arm.

"Wait," he said. "Maybe we should take both bags to Jack Frost!"

Ava and the girls glanced at each other in horror.

"Do you think so?" the goblin with Ava's bag asked doubtfully. "I think Jack Frost would like this green one the best."

"OK, then," the other goblin finally agreed.

Ava, Rachel and Kirsty breathed a sigh of relief as the goblin finally dropped Ava's bag on the path. Then the two of

them went happily on their way, taking
the green bag with them.

Laughing, Ava, Rachel and Kirsty
swooped down from the tree. Ava touched
her wand to the bag and it immediately
shrank down to fairy-size.

"Thank you so, so much, girls!" Ava
cried, hugging her magical bag happily.
"This means that sunsets all over the fairy
and human worlds can be beautiful and
colourful again. Now, you'd better get
back to Camp Stargaze."

With a wave of her wand, Ava restored
Rachel and Kirsty to their human
size. Then they hurried through the
Whispering Wood.

As they followed the path to
the campsite, Peter appeared. Ava
immediately hid in Rachel's pocket.

"Found you!" Peter exclaimed with a grin. "Everyone else is back at the camp."

Rachel and Kirsty shared a secret smile as they followed Peter along the path. When they reached the edge of the Whispering Wood, Ava fluttered out of Rachel's pocket again. Keeping out of sight of the other campers, she opened her magic bag and sprinkled a handful of shimmering golden dust in the air.

"Now you'll see what a real sunset should look like, girls!" Ava whispered,

giving them each a quick hug. "Thanks again for your help. And I know the other Twilight Fairies will be coming to see you very soon!"

And then Ava vanished, returning to Fairyland in a whirl of sparkles.

Kirsty and Rachel gazed up at the sky. All the campers, including the girls, clapped and cheered as the green sunset slowly began to fade. Soft shades of pink,

orange and gold began to appear until
the whole sky was flushed with beautiful
colour. Then the sun began to sink slowly
and steadily beyond the horizon.

"It's the end of our first day at Camp
Stargaze, Rachel," Kirsty said with a
smile.

"But it's the start of a whole new
fairy adventure!" Rachel added, her
voice full of excitement. "I wonder which
Twilight Fairy we'll meet next?"

The Twilight Fairies

Now Rachel and Kirsty have helped
Ava, it's time to help...

Lexi the Firefly Fairy

A Face in the Bushes

The sun was just setting and the evening
starting to grow chilly at Camp Stargaze.
Rachel Walker zipped up her fleece and
tucked an arm through Kirsty Tate's to
keep warm. Rachel and Kirsty were best
friends, and their families had come on
a camping holiday together for a week.
Exciting things always seemed to happen
when the two girls got together – and so
far, this holiday was already looking like
being another very magical one!

Kirsty and Rachel were gathered with
about twenty other children at the edge
of the campsite. There was going to be

a special night-time walk, and everyone was chattering excitedly as they waited to set off.

"Is everyone ready? Then let's go into the Whispering Wood!" called Peter, one of the play-leaders.

Kirsty and Rachel walked with the rest of the group into the woodland. It was cool and dark underneath the leafy trees, and Kirsty flicked on her torch and shone it around. The tall trees swayed in a gentle breeze, and their leaves really did seem to make a whispering sound. "It's creepy being here in the evening, isn't it?" she said to Rachel.

"I know," Rachel replied, glancing into the undergrowth. "Makes you wonder what's in those shadowy corners."

"Whoooo-oooo-oooo!"

Rachel and Kirsty clutched at each

other as they heard a ghostly wailing behind them. They spun round to see two boys, Lucas and Matt, laughing so hard they were bent double. "Gotcha!" Matt chortled.

"Your faces! You looked terrified!" Lucas added, his eyes sparkling with mischief.

Kirsty and Rachel laughed too, once their hearts had stopped racing. Those boys! Then Kirsty had an idea, and winked at Rachel. "Oh my goodness!" she said, pretending to gasp in fright. "Look up there – two glowing eyes staring down at us!"

The boys gazed at the tree where Kirsty was pointing – and now it was their turn to look scared. "No way!" Matt yelped in alarm. Shining out of the darkness were two gleaming lights, which looked exactly like the eyes of a wild animal. "What is it, do you reckon? A panther?"

"Hmmm," said Rachel, pretending to think. "It looks like it's a really dangerous...*firefly* or two!" She and Kirsty giggled. The glittering lights in the tree were only a couple of flickering fireflies – there was nothing scary or dangerous about *them*...

Read the rest of

Lexi
the Firefly Fairy

to find out what magic happens next...

Available now!

Florence the Friendship Fairy

978-1-40831-238-4
£5.99

Can Kirsty and Rachel find the three lost
magical items that Florence needs to keep
friendship special?

Have you checked out the

website at:
www.rainbowmagicbooks.co.uk

Meet the Showtime Fairies

out now!

Madison the Magic Show Fairy
978-1-40831-286-5

Leah the Theatre Fairy
978-1-40831-287-2

Alesha the Acrobat Fairy
978-1-40831-288-9

Darcey the Dance Diva Fairy
978-1-40831-289-6

Amelia the Singing Fairy
978-1-40831-291-9

Isla the Ice Star Fairy
978-1-40831-292-6

Taylor the Talent Show Fairy
978-1-40831-290-2